Tales From Between Presents

Ivy Grimes'
Grime Time

CONTENTS

About

Tales From Between Presents is a journal dedicated to the work of a single author each edition. This publication is edited by author and publisher, Matthew Stott.

CONTACT: frombetween@gmail.com

TWITTER: @from_between

INSTAGRAM: @tales_from_between

PATREON: Join our Patreon and support this publication. It also acts as an eBook subscription to everything we publish. Support new writing: patreon.com/TalesFromBetween

MEET THE AUTHOR

Ivy Grimes lives in Virginia, and her stories have appeared in The Baffler, Potomac Review, ergot., Vastarien, Seize the Press, South Dakota Review, and elsewhere. To read more, find her @IvyGri on Twitter and at www.ivyivyivyivy.com. For thoughts on writing and fairy tales and being scared, please visit ivygrimes.substack.com.

THE EDITOR SPEAKS

There is no easy way to describe what Ivy Grimes is able to do on the page, other than perhaps this: it's really *very* Grimesy. It's Grimesed up. Fully Grimes. If you've ever read one of her stories, I think you'll understand.

Ivy looks at the world in an odd way, and tells us what she sees with matter-of-fact humour and abundant strangeness. The first time I read her work was when she submitted a story titled *Henry's Legacy* to our Lit Journal, it featured a time-travelling Henry VIII. So. Instant acceptance, really.

I hope (demand) you enjoy this slim collection, and if you find the world a weirder place afterwards, just know that it was always so, you just needed to dip your head below the Grimes line to see it.

Speak soon, *Strangers*,
Matthew Stott, e.i.c, Tales From Between

Ms.
Dynamo

I bought one of the new AI nostalgia dolls, but I didn't do it because I missed Nick and needed company. Nick was terrible company anyway with his suggestions for changing everything about me, and with his fancy heated pajamas that turned our bed into a sauna. No, I simply wanted to enjoy myself for a change, even if it seemed childish. So I spent thousands of dollars on my very own Ms. Dynamo.

The *Ms. Dynamo Happy Hour* was my favorite show as a kid, and I thought having Ms. Dynamo around the house all day would be hilarious. I certainly didn't expect her to frighten me. After all, what's frightening about an assertive, child-sized elephant with wide lidless eyes and fluffy red hair? I was delighted at first.

When I opened her box, she stomped right out and said her signature catchphrase: "I'm going ballistic!" Then she did her famous power dance, stomping her feet while pumping her arms in the air.

It was so magical to see her dancing in my living room. It gave me the light, happy feeling of being a kid again. When I reached down to give her a hug, though, she shoved me away.

"Who are you?" she said, her pencil-thin eyebrows arching.

"I'm Eleanor. I'm...your new friend?" I didn't know how to explain I had purchased an AI version of a character on a children's show that, while still available to stream, had peaked in popularity twenty years prior. Didn't they install her with some sort of self-awareness chip? I definitely didn't want to give her an existential shock.

"Oh, so you're one of those pathetic losers who's trying to relive her youth. Right?"

"I guess so," I said, trying to laugh it off. Ms. Dynamo was sassy, after all. It was what I'd always loved about her. Sometimes I tried talking to my friends the way Ms. Dynamo talked to her friends (the sheep Ms. Ivy and the mare Mr. Oats), but it never worked. They'd ask me why I was being so mean.

I tried to banter with her for the rest of the evening, though she did hurt my feelings several times. While going through my drawers (at her insistence), she noticed an old receipt for a tie I'd bought for Nick for his birthday. It didn't take long for her to start interrogating me about him.

"Was he hot stuff? Who broke it off? Show me a picture."

I pulled out my phone—I felt I had no choice. I didn't go into the details of our breakup, but I explained that he was finally the one who dumped me. She laughed at his appearance and said that even I could do better. Sort of a compliment, right?

I knew I should cut her off, set boundaries, show her who was boss. But she was Ms. Dynamo, my childhood hero, and I'd invested so much money in her. I kept reminding myself that she wasn't really mean—she was just programmed to be that way.

And I was programmed to do what people said until I simply couldn't take it anymore. Nick's griping and criticizing had brought me to my breaking point. Ms. Dynamo was almost as critical as he was, but she had so much charisma and style. I hoped I would get used to her.

That night, I put her to bed in the guest room and set her to sleep mode. She said she shouldn't have to power down just because weak mortals had to. I was strong, though—I smiled and pressed the button anyway. I got ready for bed, basking in the peaceful silence.

Before I went to sleep, I called my Aunt Theresa to tell her about my strange new toy.

"You're just distracting yourself from your loneliness," she said. "Now you have no one."

"I have you. And my friends." My parents weren't in the picture, so Aunt Theresa had raised me. I called Theresa every other day or so, and I felt very close to her.

"But I won't be around forever. And friends are mostly there for fair weather."

"I have me, too."

It sounded so empowering when I said it, it made me feel like a feminist trailblazer of old. Aunt Theresa sighed and wished me goodnight.

Now that Nick was gone, I could luxuriate in the center of the bed and twist all the covers up in my legs. I really didn't miss him at all, though I was bitter that he had had the last word. I had just closed my eyes when I heard the toilet flush in the guest room.

"Ms. Dynamo?" I called out.

Silence.

Did AI puppets need to use the bathroom? Was that why they cost so much?

It occurred to me that someone could have broken in to steal and resell the very pricey Ms. Dynamo. Out of some manic need to protect my investment (and my new robotic friend), I jumped up, grabbed a flashlight that was heavy enough to give someone a concussion, and ran to the bathroom just as the toilet flushed again.

I caught Ms. Dynamo standing beside the toilet, watching pills swirl around on their way to the sewer. Four tiny amber prescription bottles were lined up on the edge of the tub. The bottles were empty now, but three were mine, and one was a bottle Nick had left behind. All had been stored in my bathroom. She must have crept in and taken them after I turned the lights out.

"What are you doing?"

"Destroying the evidence," she said calmly.

"This isn't evidence! This is my anxiety medication, my acne medication, my heart medication, and Nick's depression medication. I hadn't even noticed that Nick left it behind. But I need my medicines! Now I'll have to make some excuse to my doctor so I can have them refilled."

Her eyebrows rose, and she looked right at me. My inquisitor!

"I'm not a doctor, so I don't know what these medicines do," she said. "But I'm trying to help you, Eleanor. I know you killed

Nick, but I don't know how. My working theory is that you crushed a bunch of pills into his food. I'm destroying the pills before the police find them. We can destroy the bottles, too. We'll find a trash can far away to toss them into."

"What are you talking about? Nick isn't dead, and I didn't kill him! He moved an hour away to live with his mom. What the hell, Ms. Dynamo?" I decided something was wrong with her program. As much as I hated to complain, I'd have to contact the helpsite on her box. I might even have to send her back.

"You're lying," she said quietly.

Every AI I encountered in my everyday life was reliable, from the calm headless dentist AI that examined my teeth to the smiling clerk AI at the grocery store. Maybe they weren't good in any philosophical sense, but they were entirely trustworthy. I'd always thought that people who were anti-AI were anti-progress, mere conspiracy theorists. Yet here I was, in possession of a robot that was trying to drive me mad.

"Why don't you go back to bed?" I said, feeling helpless. I doubted she would stand idly by while I found a way to get her back in her box and return her. The drone who'd delivered her wouldn't be back to my house until morning. Worst of all, I'd feel terrible for abandoning her. Maybe I could make the best of things and enjoy her for the remainder of the night. The loss of my medicine was annoying, but there wasn't much of value in my house that she could destroy. My splurging on Ms. Dynamo was a rare thing.

"I'm not sleepy," she said, and crossed her arms. I couldn't help but laugh at her childlike insouciance.

"The ads show people braiding your hair and having sleep-overs with you. We could have some fun. You could even stay in my bed if you're lonely. What do you say?"

"Hmm," she murmured as she turned to face the empty pill bottles. "But then who would finish destroying the evidence? There are loads of suspicious things around here. The police are sure to investigate any moment. Even purchasing me was suspicious! You probably bought me with life insurance money. Didn't you?"

"Ha!" I gently grabbed her shoulder and led her to my bedroom. I grabbed a brush from my bedside table and began to brush her hair, hoping it would soothe her. Soothe a robot! I wasn't thinking rationally.

"Why did you do it, Eleanor?"

"Ms. Dynamo! How many times do I have to tell you? I didn't do anything. I didn't kill Nick. He's still alive!"

"Then call him."

"He's asleep. And we aren't on speaking terms anyway. He won't answer, but that doesn't mean he's dead."

She chuckled. She asked for my phone and entered the password—which of course I hadn't given her—and did a search for Nick. To my surprise, his picture showed up on a statewide missing person's alert.

A shock of terror ran through me, followed by a perverse sense of joy. Maybe he'd been attacked by muggers on the way to his mom's, or maybe his car had crashed and landed in some hidden ditch. He'd been so horrible to me. I could think of worse things that had happened to better people. I know those thoughts seem awful, but that was just one train of thought I had. I also thought about our tender moments and his small kindnesses to me, and about how I didn't want anyone to suffer. Not ever.

"Oh, Ms. Dynamo. It breaks my heart that something could have happened to Nick," I said. Maybe I was oversimplifying or even exaggerating my grief, but who could blame me? I was still processing, and those are the kinds of things people say when something goes wrong.

"You're not a bad actress, kid. I should have had you on my show," she said, turning her back to me again. I kept brushing her hair, needing something to do with my hands. Since she wasn't staring at me with her beady eyes, I felt like I could relax a little. I was able to cry, to release my anxiety.

"I guess I should call his mom," I said once I had a chance to think. "I should tell her what time he left my house. Maybe we can put our heads together, figure out what happened to him."

"Don't you think the police are using their own expertise right now? Don't you think they're thinking of everything?" Her voice was so shrill and childish, yet everything she said was so wise.

I closed my eyes and remembered an old episode of *Ms. Dynamo* where she and Ms. Ivy and Mr. Oats were captured by a country man with a mullet who wanted to put them in a petting zoo. Ms. Dynamo had gone ballistic, but it hadn't helped. The country man had them all caught up in a giant net. Ms. Dynamo tried impressing him with her beautiful red hair and her shapely gray limbs. Again, her efforts were fruitless—the man had no romantic interest in elephants. Finally, she cooked up a more complicated plan. She and her friends called out to their frenemy Mr. Demon (the crow) and asked him to release his waste on the country man's head. While the country man was washing out his mullet, Mr. Demon helped chew the net to free them.

I suppose the lesson of the episode was that sometimes you have to work with people you don't like. I was beginning to dislike Ms. Dynamo, but she was so strong and clever. As Nick's ex-girlfriend, I was probably the prime suspect. Why hadn't the police contacted me? Maybe they were quietly observing me—trying to draw me out, to trip me up.

"Oh, Ms. Dynamo," I said, beginning to panic. "Ms. Dynamo!" She turned around and patted my knee. "There, there, dear. I'll take care of everything. Just stay out of the way, and let me go to work."

"I can help! I mean, what do I do? The police are sure to be after me! But I swear I didn't do it!" I was beginning to hyperventilate a little.

Ms. Dynamo rushed into the kitchen and brought me a pint of ice cream I didn't know I'd stowed away in the freezer, and she told me to rest and relax. Not many people had taken care of me in my life. Aunt Theresa was really the only one, and she was old now, close to death. I knew I couldn't call her and burden her with my problems, and none of my friends would believe what had happened to me. Anyway, the police were probably listening to my calls.

As I ate my ice cream, I tried to clear my mind. Ms. Dynamo put some gentle classical music on the sound system, and I felt my head get lighter and lighter.

"Ms. Dynamo?" I called out. "What did you put in my ice cream?"

I was asleep before she could answer.

When I woke up, I knew it was later in the morning than I usually opened my eyes. Fortunately, it was a Friday, so I was off of work. My mouth tasted funny and dry, and I looked over at the empty carton of ice cream on my bedside table and felt confused. I normally didn't eat in bed. Nick had absolutely forbidden it. He always said calories consumed while lying down were impossible to burn.

Slowly, it all came back to me. Nick was *gone*. Missing. Possibly dead. I'd bought a Ms. Dynamo AI, and she was loose in my house, "destroying evidence." Although I was still woozy, I shot out of bed and went from room to room in search of her gray form.

Everything was neat on the surface, but I could tell it had all been touched. When I opened a drawer, its contents were tidier than they had been before. The towels in my bathrooms were slightly rearranged. In the kitchen, the cans and boxes had been put in the wrong cabinets. Worst of all, when I reached the living room and found Ms. Dynamo, she was sitting on the couch, having tea with a police officer.

"Oh God!" I said, pulling my bathrobe tight around my waist, embarrassed for the man to see my pink pajamas.

"Please don't be alarmed," he said. "I'm just responding to a friendly call from Ms. Dynamo."

She turned to me, an empty teacup in her lap.

"Why would you believe a doll?" I asked the officer, my voice trembling. "You're having an imaginary tea party with her the way little kids do."

I felt like I might be going ballistic. Ms. Dynamo had clearly set me up. She'd made me paranoid, tried to get a confession out of me, and had called the police to search my apartment while I was asleep.

"Shut up!" she said to me, her eyebrows contracting into a cute little frown. "I'm not a doll. I'm a very intelligent person. You see, I was explaining to this nice policeman that Nick has gone missing. We just found out, or we would have reported it sooner. But this nice officer here has been telling me how Nick was found last night, picked up by a trucker and taken to a police station. Fortunate, isn't it?"

She uncrossed and recrossed her legs while giving the officer a winsome smile. I sat down beside her and tried to calm down. This was too much—to have lost my relationship with Nick, then lost him entirely, only to have him turn up again.

"Yes, we've been having a great time talking together. I've always loved Ms. Dynamo's show," the officer said. He was a tall and jolly man who didn't seem to mind that I had compared him to a small child. "As I was telling Ms. Dynamo, there's no need to fret. Your boyfriend—or former boyfriend—was discovered last night. He hitchhiked to the lake for a fishing trip, and he hadn't told his mom, who was expecting him home. He said he needed to get a bad taste out of his mouth, and he didn't owe it to his mother or any woman be where she wanted him to be. Kind of a nasty character, that one. He was picked up by a trucker who'd seen the missing persons alert, and in the end, your fellow felt foolish for giving everyone a scare. I think he's learned his lesson."

I was relieved for a moment, but a sense of unease crept into my chest. Was Nick really still alive, or was this part of the policeman's plan to extract a confession from me? The moment I saw the alert that Nick was missing, I had a feeling he was dead. I sort of sensed that his spirit had vacated the earth. But I knew I hadn't killed him. It was impossible to kill someone and forget it, wasn't it?

"Well...thank you for the information," I said, trying to smile at the man.

Ms. Dynamo changed the subject to talk about the new uniforms police were wearing these days and how handsome they were. They looked like butcher's white coats, but they had festive orange stripes.

"So lovely! And they're safer for night patrols. You're much more visible that way." She was able to smile at him the whole time she was talking. It was an advantage that her cheeks never got tired.

"And they're temperature-controlled!" the officer bragged, patting his warm pockets.

They went on like this for another few minutes, and then the officer said he had to get back to work.

"Come by anytime!" Ms. Dynamo said, with one eyebrow raised suggestively.

The officer thought this was hilarious, and he promised to give us a visit in the future.

We stood outside and waved to him as he walked away, and then Ms. Dynamo pulled me back inside. I had no idea her little arms were so strong.

"You're utterly incompetent!" she shouted once she'd closed the door and dragged me into the kitchen. "You almost bungled my perfect plan!"

"What plan? Why don't I get to know the plans?"

"Because you're incompetent! You'd bungle my plans even worse if you understood them! You're as bad as Ms. Ivy and Mr. Oats. See, I needed the police to know we were concerned about Nick's absence so they'd think we were worried about him. Meanwhile, the Nick they found isn't the boring old soft-organed Nick you know. I called in a favor at the factory. You know, the one where I was born."

"So...the new Nick is a...?"

"Yes, he's like me. Don't worry. His mother will never notice. No one will ever notice. They sculpted his face perfectly, and they'll summon him in for alterations as he ages. They programmed him to be ornery. In fact, if you start to miss him, I can have him summoned here for you. I don't recommend it, though. Better to make a clean break and move oh, eh?"

"Oh, but Ms. Dynamo! I promise I didn't kill Nick. I truly don't know what happened to him."

She smiled at me. "It doesn't matter, Eleanor. What matters is that it's all taken care of. I know I can be hasty sometimes, but I always figure out the right answer in the end. Don't you worry. I'm going to be taking care of everything from now on. You'll have the most wonderful time."

My head was still woozy from whatever she'd put in my ice cream. When she told me to take a shower and get dressed, I did as she said. Once I was alone in the shower, I let myself shed a few tears, though I didn't know if they were tears of joy or sorrow.

Either way, it didn't matter. Ms. Dynamo would know. Perhaps one day she'd trust me enough of me to tell me what had happened and how I was supposed to feel about it.

Originally Published in Dark Matter Magazine

Author Note:

My childhood heroes were often aggressive in ways I wouldn't let myself be. As I wrote this story, I was thinking about how funny and annoying and necessary it is to be in the presence of stubborn people who won't listen. On the other hand, it's also tiring, especially if the stubborn person is you...eventually you have to separate that part of yourself and give them an off switch. I look forward to having headless AI dentists someday, too.

Hitchcock

S carecrow is what I call the dead actor, my old friend. He worked for me in the old days, and we work together now. Together, we make shadows.

"I played shadows my whole life," he tells me. "I can't stop now."

It is dangerous to love a job so much.

I murder a farmer who is holding his rake in the sky in a gesture of defiance. Scarecrow doesn't watch the blood seep into the hot dirt. He stands where the farmer once stood and lifts his arm into the sky and distorts his hand into the shape of a rake. Don't look right at him! That would be like looking into the sun. Look at the shadow he casts. He recreates the shadow of the farmer holding the rake. Perfectly. What an artist.

He accuses me of murdering the farmer to give him work, and he thanks me.

I cause an accident on the corner of Turner and Ash. Late at night, a driver weaves through an empty street, and I pull my car in front of his in the intersection. Together, we crash into the street sign marking Turner in one direction and Ash in the other, and the sign topples. There is no more shadow of the street sign.

I stay in my car and pretend to be unconscious. The man in the other car is unconscious. Scarecrow has the privacy to slip into place, and he multiplies his arms and arranges them into a beautiful shape (I take one peek, but you shouldn't), and on the ground, he makes a shadow exactly like a street sign (and a broken cross). Scarecrow empathizes with shadows, and so he is the best.

I try to lure Scarecrow into my home by breaking lamps that cast unusual shadows, but he won't venture indoors. He speaks to me on my lawn and thanks me for all the roles I've given him.

"I've seen you make shadows in life and death, and you are the greatest," I tell him. I have a reputation for honesty. I never flatter.

"I don't want to be just any shadow," he says. "I want a real challenge now."

All of us want challenges—to feel we've run the race. To hear the Lord say, "Well done." Do you believe that if you do your job well that you will be rewarded?

There are saints who receive rewards in heaven, I have no doubt. But they are not masters of their craft.

I give Scarecrow a challenge—the last I am able to give him. I remove my shadow by removing my own body. When I am gone, he contorts himself into a horrible shape—but on the ground it is the perfect shadow. It is my shadow—the very shadow I once cast. Others might imitate, but no one can replicate shadows like Scarecrow can.

Now that I am bodiless, I follow him everywhere. Together, we pass time making perfect shapes. If one of the living looks up at an ill-timed moment, they get a terrible shock. If you are alive, you are our audience.

Keep your eyes on the shadows. That is where our souls are. That is where the only beauty is.

Originally Published in ergot.

Author Note:

In my nightmare, Jimmy Stewart was a scarecrow who pointed towards cornfields and bookstores that sold evil board games. He wanted me to find creepy fun. I must have had the dream in the fall.

I wouldn't want to direct. You place bets with your actions. What if, in life or death, we eventually understand the pain we cause? In the meantime, you can understand why some people want to make shadows. I like to look to see how they did the trick, which gives me nightmares.

Questions

& Answers

What is your favourite part of the writing process?
The idea stage!

You have set up home (online, at least) in the horror genre, even though your stories are often not really horror-specific. As a writer of strange stories, did you find it tricky trying to define what you are and where best to place yourself?

I didn't set out to place myself anywhere in particular. I wrote poetry earlier in life, so I got used to feeling like no one was paying attention to what I was doing anyway. (I'd like to write more poetry at some point, but I haven't felt the spark to do so lately.) Some of my main inspirations are somewhat horrific, though. I feel most excited when I'm writing in the vein of Lynch, Kafka, Murakami, and Beckett...with healthy dashes of other scary stuff like sitcoms and Hallmark movies and reality TV. I'm also a longtime fan of Flannery O'Connor and Shirley Jackson.

I'm not an expert on what the genre is or what it should be. I don't want to disappoint hardcore fans who open a horror magazine seeking gore and instead find my story about a mildly threatening man at a grocery store! I want them to know I'm writing something more absurdist and eerie than truly bone-chilling so they don't waste their time or money. Right now, we're grouping this eerie stuff under "weird fiction" or "strange fiction," which falls under the broader horror umbrella. I would rather someone else solve the problem of how to classify the work!

What is your least favourite part of the writing process?
The proofreading and releasing it into the world stage.

Your writing often has a comedic edge to it, which I really like and think helps your writing stand out; did you always intend to have humour in your stories, and where do you think that desire originates?
I'm reminded of my Grandfather Grimes, who always had the perfect joke in response to every annoyance and insult (whether actual or perceived). He kept his cool that way. Really, there are a lot of people in my family like this. Without being able to joke about my grievances (again, actual or perceived), I'd have to start lifting weights, because I'd be getting into fistfights. Some funny writers I admire are Flannery O'Connor, Lorrie Moore, Allen Ginsberg, Ralph Ellison, Kurt Vonnegut, Richard Brautigan, Raymond Carver, Raymond Chandler, Brandon Taylor, Barbara Pym, Barbara Comyns, Mary Karr, and our friend Shirley Jackson (among many others).

Who is your favourite author/authors and why?

Every author I've mentioned throughout this interview! Additionally, I love the musty classics like Dickens and Austen and Dostoevsky. I also love Tove Jansson, Iris Murdoch, James Joyce, Toni Morrison, Donna Tartt, Kazuo Ishiguro, Leonora Carrington, Henri Nouwen, Paul Auster, Hilary Mantel, Joy Williams, Alice Munro, Tana French, Maya Angelou, Virginia Woolf, and so on forever. And too many new writers to name.

I am not sure what draws us to some writers and not to others. I think it's like friendship, though. There are some we feel close to right away and others we struggle to understand.

What/who do you think influences your work?

I feel very influenced by the writers I love, the ones listed previously in this interview and many others. And new writers. Plenty of other forms of storytelling, too.

Since I grew up in the Bible Belt, that influences my stories in many ways. I especially feel the storytelling influence of *Genesis*, which is funny and strange and deeply sad. Unfortunately, the US has too many leaders who seem uninterested in poetry or history or reading in context, and they bypass the complexity of these stories to use them to deny scientific discoveries and to shape discriminatory public policy. And that's been true for some time, especially in the South, a place I love in so many other ways! But I digress.

Anyway, along the same lines, I love parables and koans, mysteries that can't be solved. Also, fairy tales and folklore and folk songs are important to me. In general, I love stories passed down by people who weren't writing anything down, but were living with those stories day-to-day and letting the days shape them.

Plenty of people in my family are storytellers as well, and they've all influenced me.

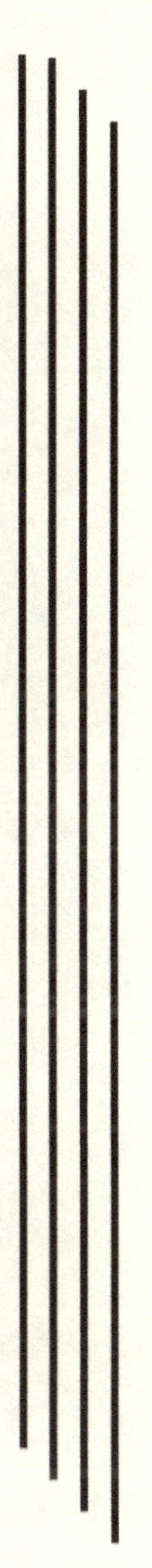

The
Arcade

I had to take a trip with everyone. We all met on the beach every day and chatted about awkward topics. I stayed in a house with my whole extended family, mostly people I felt no connection to. You have to do things like that sometimes, and there's no way out. It's the social contract.

The only way for me to survive was to stay up all night and sleep through most of the day. That way, I could spend less time with everyone.

So every night, I watched old movies on my phone in the relative privacy of my room. People kept coming in and out since I had one of the rare bedrooms with an attached bathroom. They paused on the way to or from the bathroom to look over my shoulder, aghast at how I was spending our beach trip.

Aunt Ann said: "We're supposed to use this time."

Great-Uncle Gordon said: "That movie sucks."

My sister said: "Why are you withdrawing into yourself?"

My mom said: "Beach trips are about beach time!"

I muttered something to make them go away, kept watching my movies, and slept dutifully through the mornings, no matter how much noise everyone made. Due to the social contract, they weren't allowed to punch me awake.

It was an imperfect life, but it was a way to avoid something worse.

I was excited at first, I admit, when two new girls appeared in our beach house. They were young, maybe in their 20s. One had pink hair, and the other had blue. They were not part of my family, and no one could remember inviting them. I met them on a sunny afternoon when I ventured from my room to get food while everyone else was still at the beach. They were laughing with each other in the living room. I was so surprised, I stumbled over a footstool on my way to get a closer look. The pink one stared at me, and the blue one laughed. I was tempted to run back to my room and hate them for the rest of the trip or the rest of my life, whichever ended first. I waited, though, because of how they looked at me.

"You have a beautiful aura," the pink one said.

I was flattered. No one had said anything like that to me before. Everyone at the beach house thought I was awful.

"Do you know who I am?" I said. I hadn't introduced my-self.

They nodded.

"Are you in my family?"

They shook their heads.

"Then why are you here? Who invited you?"

"Our friends at the arcade told us to come," the blue one said.

"We're here to help," the pink one said.

That was all they could explain. I didn't want to annoy them the way my family annoyed me (by asking too many questions).

Still, I couldn't help but ask, "What did you mean about my aura?"

I wondered if they had tools with them, sun charts and symbols. I needed some signs, and in fact I'd been praying for signs. Maybe that was why I was watching those old movies. All the chattering on the beach and in the beach house had taught me nothing.

The pink girl waved her hands around her face. "Right there," she said. "It's beautiful."

"What do I do about it?" I said.

She looked at me a little too long. "We'll have to wait and see."

From then on, my plans became more complicated. I was never alone in the beach house. When my family was out, the girls were in. When my family was in, they were gone. I could never be really alone, and I was losing my mind. I started hiding in the shower since the bathroom was the one place with a door that locked.

I could hear my family gossiping about me. Through the closed door, I heard them wondering what was wrong with me and what to do about me. They hoped the arcade girls would help. If I had been in the mood to join the conversation, I would have told them not to hold their breaths.

And yet. Maybe the girls could help me if they had the right knowledge. I kept thinking of how to surprise them, how to corner them, how to casually ask all the questions I had. Was your aura the same thing as your spirit? What was a spirit? What wisdom could come through signs and wonders?

So as discreetly as I could, I started following them. I used my beach time to sneak away from the sand and over to the beachside arcade, hoping to run into them. I couldn't ask them questions in the beach house. It wasn't the right place.

At the beach house, the walls were made of gray granite, and hard little seats were carved in the stone. People sat in those seats whenever they had arguments so that they could say everything they were thinking instead of walking away in disgust.

Every day, my father and great-grandfather would get into an argument over whose business had been the most prosperous, and the house would draw them magnetically to the granite walls where they had to sit and talk about it until they stopped arguing. It made me feel cold to see them sitting side by side, gripping their gray granite armrests. Neither of them had bank books or accountants at the beach with them, so it was a fight that could never be won. At any given moment when my family wasn't at the beach, someone was bound to the walls, arguing. It only happened to me once when I made the mistake of participating in an argument with my granddaughter about the merits of lizards. I felt I had to defend them. Never again did I make that mistake. I let the lizards defend the lizards.

If I was going to argue with the blue girl and pink girl, it would have to be in the arcade. And I knew we would argue, because I was tired of being nice.

Inside the arcade, the giant room was lit by game screens and neon strips. The floor was sand. The workers wore white smocks with red stripes. I found the girls playing a game called

Spool: How I Made a Million in Thread. The blue one played while the pink one watched, and I stood behind them so that they weren't aware of me. With a joystick, you made a person walk around a warehouse full of thread. The warehouse reminded me of the arcade. You had to work filling orders for people. Purple, chartreuse, platinum. The challenge of the game seemed to be color detection. I would have lost, because I can't distinguish between shades of the same shade.

I realized the blue one was going to play the game all day with her friend looking on, so I knew I had to intervene to make my case. I tapped her on the shoulder while she was trying to find the rust thread.

"What the hell?" she said, flipping around, tossing her blue hair in my face.

The pink one watched us. She didn't get mad.

"You have to help me," I said.

"We're trying to! You make it hard," the blue one said.

"Please tell me what my aura is. It needs to be something more specific than beautiful. It might seem vain or silly, but I have to know. Once I know what my aura is, I think I can move into my own beach house, and then I could help people like me."

"What are you talking about?" the blue one said. She snickered at me. "You're on vacation. You can't help anyone with anything."

"What exactly are you helping with?" I said.

"We're watching you," she said, as if that explained anything.

"We come to help people who aren't enjoying their beach trips," the pink one said. She was kinder, but not much more articulate.

"So you are in the beach house because of me? Well, what have you done to help me enjoy things?"

"She already told you. We watch until we know how to help. You're a tough code to crack," the blue one said. "You don't seem to care about anything, so what can we use as leverage?"

I rolled my eyes. "It's so obvious! You could use old movies. That's what I spend the most time with. You could pick out old movies for me to watch that would teach me whatever lesson I need to learn to help me enjoy the beach trip. You could ask me leading questions about the movies I watch until I have some kind of epiphany. If you cared at all about your jobs, and about me, then you would have already realized that."

"Movies are boring!" the blue one said. "You should play arcade games instead. I know all about those."

The pink-haired girl put her hand on my shoulder. "You're right," she said. "I'll watch some old movies so I can explain things to you."

"You have to meet us halfway, though," the blue one said. "Play some games for us."

I stayed in the arcade the rest of the day and played a game called *Blaze* where I chased a little ball of fire around with a bucket of water. I wasted a lot of water, and I never put the blaze out. It was kind of addicting, though, so I stayed for hours and hours.

Exhausted, I returned to the beach house just as the sun was setting, slipping past a gaggle of aunts who were standing in the doorway and talking about skirt lengths. I ignored their questions about where I'd been and how I was feeling and hurried away to my room. I was pretty sure that if I gave in and joined their conversation, I'd die of boredom. And if I died at the beach house, where would I go? There was no hospital at the beach. No funeral home.

The movie I'd planned to watch first that night was called *Sun Runes*, but I felt my head grow heavy. I closed my eyes for what felt like a minute, and when I woke up, the pink light of sunrise was streaming through my window. My bedroom door flew open, and I closed my eyes again, pretending to sleep so I wouldn't have to speak to the family member headed for the bathroom.

But someone started shaking me, and when I opened my eyes, I saw the blue-haired girl jostling me while the pink-haired girl stood back and watched.

"Hey, that's rude!" I said.

"I'm rude," the blue one said. The pink one smiled a sweet pixie smile, and I decided to relax.

"Are you going to help me out with your arcane wisdom? Maybe tell me how a beautiful aura will help me in my present situation?" I said.

"Okay, but tell us something first. Have you ever seen an old movie about a man who sells sandwiches on a train, and he's so clumsy that he manages to stop a robbery?" the blue one said.

"Hmm," I said, searching my memory.

"He keeps falling everywhere," the pink one said. "He accidentally runs his cart over the robber's foot."

"Yeah, I do think I've seen that one. What about it?" I said.

"We think we understand you now. You're not cruel. You're just doing something different than the rest of your family. They're on a train, and you're trying to rob it," the blue one said.

"I don't want anything from anyone!" I protested. What could they have that I would want to rob?

"Well, we're selling sandwiches. But we need to be a little clumsier," the pink one said. She was so gentle and pleasant. I wondered why she put up with the other one.

"How so?"

Instead of answering me, they pulled me up and dragged me out to the kitchen where the earliest risers in my family were having breakfast. My grandmother was there with her aunt and my cousin Andy and my second-cousin Preston and a few other people whose names I didn't know, and they were all having Denver omelets.

"Good Lord!" Preston said. "She's alive! Here, have an omelet."

Before I could run away, the pink-haired girl intervened for me. "Don't you see that she doesn't want to be here?"

All my family members present looked blankly at me.

"Doesn't want to be on our beach trip?" my grandmother said, her voice quavering a little.

I ducked my head. "I don't like it here," I admitted.

One of my relatives whose name I had forgotten (or never learned) looked at me with dismay. "Why?" she said. She was just a kid.

"I don't know." I needed something to do with my hands, so I grabbed a plate and an omelet from the buffet and sat at the huge kitchen table, as far away from the others as I could get. The blue-haired and pink-haired girls hovered over me, refusing to sit.

"She wants to be free," the blue one said.

No one looked me in the eye.

"Well," my grandmother said. "If that's what she wants..."

I gasped. It felt like a row of heavy war medals had fallen from my chest, and I was light enough to pick myself up again. I could stand so easily.

"I can leave?" I said.

"Who's going to stop you?" said the kid whose name I didn't know. She smirked at me like she didn't think I was very smart.

So what, though? Now I could leave, and I didn't have to worry about what any of them said about me.

By the time I'd waved goodbye and wished all present well and promised to see everyone at the beach, the blue one was at the door with my packed suitcase, and the pink one was pulling me away. We walked out the front door, and I felt like I'd grown the helpful tools of beasts...tusks and wings and flippers. I felt like I could rise into the air or dive deep into the sea. Or fight.

"Where are we going now?" I said.

"Where do you want to go?" the pink one said.

There wasn't anywhere to go except the beach and the arcade. Between the two, I chose the arcade.

I ordered a hot dog and watched some kids play a game called *Finance: Exchange Rates*. I told the pink and blue one I thought it was boring.

"Come play *Spool*!" the pink one urged me.

I was having a good time, and I was grateful to them, so I agreed. I sat down at the game and started playing while the girls watched me. I was terrible at the game. It asked me to find champagne thread, and I found ecru. It asked me to find forget-me-not thread, and I found baby blue. I hated the game! I gave it a warning kick.

"Don't you see, though?" the blue one said.

"That I'm bad at colors?" I said.

"No. Something else," the pink one said.

I stared at them as a line formed behind us to use the game.

"Does it have to do with my aura?" I said.

But they wouldn't answer me. I moved so someone else could use the game.

I went to the arcade bathroom to freshen up. It was full of people doing their makeup and reading books and making paper airplanes and stuff. I washed my face with cheap hand soap, and I felt like I was young again. I felt like I had years to play, to be someone I hadn't quite been.

"Nice color!" I told the old woman beside me who was painting her eyelids mint green.

She smiled. "You too. A beautiful shade of moss."

I wasn't wearing makeup, so she must have meant the color of my aura. I went back out to choose a new game and noticed that the blue-haired and pink-haired girl were back at the *Spool* game. The blue one was as determined as a bull, and the pink one was laughing and clapping. I sat down at a game called *Remember the Time*. I played a kid who was on vacation at the beach, running away from crabs and trying to build sand castles. I got pretty good at the game by the time the sun set. I wasn't tired at all, so I played the game all night, and in the morning, I bought doughnuts to share with the girls.

Author Note:

I think you have a beautiful aura, too!

Glass
House

M y house decided it was time to go underground. I made the birds and beasts jealous by living in a nest of the shrugged-off skins of angels. Maybe angels were jealous of me, too. But no one wanted to live like me.

In their ignorance, people want to live within layers of marble and gold. They miss being fetal, so they curl up and cover themselves in opaque shells.

But I want to see through, even now. Through my glass walls, I see packed earth and roots and curling worms. Through the soil, the breaths come: breaths of hot winds fog my walls, and breaths of ice leave tributaries of frost.

I conjure my own sun in the kitchen to warm my cheeks while I knead dough. I make gray clouds cluster over my chair as I write verses. If my glass house never rises, and if no one ever finds me, I will send my verses into people's dreams, and they will wake up singing about me.

The old druids who went before me became trees that can never be cut. They keep old wisdom in their sleeping core while their branches and roots receive news of the world. But they cannot read.

I have thousands of books (scribbled on the scabs of trees), some in dead languages I am resurrecting. I dream, but I never sleep.

In my dreams, I am a wren. Like him, I was once ruler of winter and ruler of the hedge. When I look at a tree, I can see into its heartwood where it keeps the marks of every season. As a wren, I visit my old friends.

The king and queen are dead in tombs of gold and marble. My old students are buried in humbler materials, and they are dissolving into dirt. They are lucky.

My only living friends are the trees. I nest in their branches, and through my feathers, I can feel the real sun and rain. My nest is protected by lightning. If you reach in to harm me, it will be your end.

This is not a glass prison, but if it were, I am free in my dreams. This is not a tomb, but if it were, I would be safe. This house is sacred and hard. Once it showed me the beauty of the trees and sky, and now it shows me the beauty of the loamy dark.

Author Note:

A couple of years ago, I started writing stories about glass. Glass is an invisible boundary. Glass holds you in place without obstructing your view. My hope in life is to find some sliver of enlightenment, though it is unlikely to happen to me. I can hope, though, still. When I wrote this story, I was thinking about Merlin.

Questions

&
Answers

When do you write?

I don't have a set schedule. Sometimes I'll write early in the morning for a few weeks, and then I might not write consistently for a couple of months. I like to vary my routines so I don't get bored or feel like it's a chore. But I know different methods work for different people.

Do you approach the writing of short and longer works in the same way, or is there a difference?

Before attempting something longer, I do a lot of prewriting. I journal about what I'm trying to say and who my characters are. I tend not to do this for short stories. With short stories, I can usually walk right in and make myself at home. I think most people attempting something long, particularly novel-length, end up fighting more gremlins of insecurity. This can happen with short stories too, of course. When I first started writing short stories, I'd stop at least once in the middle and consider quitting because I felt like I'd lost my map. Now I have a better sense of when it's really time to quit, and when I should press on.

The unconscious mind weaves its own webs while we aren't paying attention. I think that if anyone who loves writing keeps writing, they'll look back on old things they've written and find wonderful connections that were accidental. The trouble we tend to face as writers is that we know we can't accomplish all we want with our own intelligence. But fortunately, we don't have to.

Are there any genres or styles of stories that you shy away from writing?

I love reading elaborate, vivid prose as well as short, snippy prose...I like it all. But I write in short sentences. It's in my nature. What can you do?

What is the starting point of a story for you? A central idea, a character, a 'feel', even? Or something else?

My favorite starting point is to take something from a dream...then I get into a mood where it's like I'm dreaming while writing. That's what happened with my story "Hitch-cock." Sometimes I'll just think, "Wouldn't it be funny if..." and start there. Most often, I start with a central idea, one that explores something that I find very frightening, like the idea of doing something horrible and forgetting about it, or about being disliked and not knowing why.

Self-promotion seems to be a big part of an author's career these days, are you conscious of having to push yourself out into the world and make yourself seen? Is that something you feel adept at?

No, I do not enjoy that part of it. I want to connect with other writers, though, especially ones who are exploring the same side streets that I am. And I'm a reader, so I love connecting with other readers. I also want my work to find readers who will enjoy it.

But I don't want to waste the time of readers who won't enjoy it, so I don't want to blast my message out to the whole world. I don't want to be intrusive!

How do you feel about rejections? Do they sting or are you able to brush them off?

I've received like a million rejections at this point, so they're nothing unusual. I expect to be rejected when I send things off. I wouldn't say they sting very much. My experience of being a first reader at various places has been that there isn't enough time for the person rejecting your work to really think about it or understand it, so it seems like an impersonal process to me, one that's based on a quick gut reaction. Acceptances also don't make me feel validated as a writer, because I know it's a very subjective process, and it doesn't mean anything grand about my skills. Some acceptances make me feel lucky, though, and some rejections make me feel unlucky. No one's luck is all good or all bad, though, and it's funny how quickly our perspective can change on our own luck.

Have you always been attracted to dark stories?

Yes and no! I was always fascinated by horror, but I was so frightened that I shied away from it for a long time. It's that much more powerful to me, though, because I still truly fear some very common horror elements.

Picturing
Her
Hands

At first, Two didn't notice the tattoos on her hands. When she woke, her mind was tousled. The night had teased her with phantom smells while she was sleeping: the chemical candy of discount shower gel and the coconut plastic of a lawn chair smeared with suntan lotion and the purple whiff of fruitless juice mixed from a powder—scents she hadn't been exposed to in over a decade. The only dream she remembered was of watching a bat in the daytime furiously clawing at the wooden birdhouse where it wanted to sleep. The birdhouse entry had been boarded over while the bat was away, and the bat couldn't seem to give up on his former dwelling.

She was distracted by the memory of the fearsome bat as she rose from bed and sat on her plush window seat for several minutes, looking out on the morning fog collecting in the high trees on the edge of the estate. It was only when she washed her face that she looked down and noticed that her hands were covered with markings, strange and colorful tattoos. She was horrified and tried to think of an explanation for how her hands had been tattooed without her knowledge. As she began to panic, she heard a buzzer signaling that Helen, her maid, wanted to deliver her breakfast tray. She hurriedly returned beneath the sheets and called out that she was awake. As Helen opened the door and approached with the breakfast tray, Two quickly pulled the sleeves of her robe over her hands.

"Are you cold?" asked Helen, who was beautiful and imperious with prematurely gray hair and a lineless face. Once she had deposited the breakfast tray, she crouched to stoke the fire she had started before Two was awake, a fire that had settled into itself and lost its pop and power.

"Thank you, Helen. I'm very cold today. I had bad dreams last night."

"Dreams don't change your temperature. What can I do for you?"

"Nothing. You can go now, Helen. Thank you."

Once she was alone again, she rushed to the window to examine her hands in the gray morning light. Her eyes seemed to fill with sand so that her glimpse of the tattoos was blurred. She wasn't ready to see what they were, but she forced herself to try. The first tattoo that came into focus ran the length of her left thumb—a large, grimacing hawk wearing a bright green football helmet. Her eye was also drawn to an asterisk taking up a small amount of space in a corner of the back of her right hand. The rest of the flesh on the back of that hand was covered with a night sky in shades of newsprint with white, eight-pointed stars and gold sparkles. How utterly awful. She hated sports, and she hated this gaudy depiction of night. She had never considered getting a tattoo before. Had she been drugged or lost her mind the night before and run into town to find a tattoo parlor? It was impossible. Helen was there, for one thing, and would have noticed if she had left the house. Mother had left unusually late the night before, around nine in the evening. Two remembered going to bed just after, reading for an hour before falling asleep. When she had fallen asleep, her hands had been completely normal. Pictureless.

Was there a tattoo shop in town? She assumed so but wasn't sure. Helen shopped for food (she assumed), and clothiers and doctors and decorators came to the estate to deliver their services. Mother took care of any other rare errands.

Two's days were dull and ran together, but they were meticulously planned and organized. Two had lunch and dinner every day with Mother. Never breakfast. To Two's relief, Mother liked to sleep late and have a single cup of coffee before dressing and walking the short distance to Two's house. This had been the routine for the past seven years since Two had been married: Mother arrived around noon, Two's cook prepared whatever dish Mother had requested earlier that week, and Two and Mother discussed the décor and upkeep of the estate throughout the afternoon. After dinner, Mother went home to sleep. In the mornings, Two woke up early to read the newspaper or walk through her garden, and in the unsupervised evenings, she stared out of her window and daydreamed or read novels. Her husband had departed for a business trip after their honeymoon, and he hadn't returned. He sent her letters every week, and all of them expressed fondness for her and regret that his business abroad was so long and intricate. Each week, on the day after the letter arrived, Mother asked for news of Two's husband. That was the only time they ever talked about him.

Mother wouldn't approve of the tattoos, not at all. If Mother saw the tattoos, she would find some way to punish her. Maybe she would report the matter to Two's husband. Maybe he would divorce her and kick her out of the estate. Two checked her watch. It was eight o'clock, a few hours before Mother would arrive. Two hoped she had enough time to run to town and do something to remove the tattoos. As she contemplated her exit, she realized how strange it would be to venture outside the estate after those seven years within it.

Before she could talk herself out of leaving, Two changed into the dress Helen had laid out for her, slipped on her white fur-trimmed gloves, grabbed one of the handbags she never used, and slipped silently down the stairs. Helen would be outside directing the gardener. To escape unnoticed, Two walked quietly through the kitchen door and took the humblest stone path to the edge of the spacious yard. She passed through the wrought iron gate that was usually shut and locked but open in the morning for Mother and the gardener. Once she was outside the property, she ran. Fortunately, Mother's house was to the left, farther from the town, isolated in a little patch of woods. Two went right. She followed the small two-lane road lined with tall trees whose leaves were shockingly yellow and short, squat trees whose leaves were brown shells rattling in the wind. Only squirrels darted crossways over the road, and she met no people.

Mother had told her that some people in town were dangerous. Two had never gone against Mother's advice since Mother seemed so sure of what was out there. Some ambiguous martyrdom seemed to await her in town, but to disappoint Mother was even worse. She wouldn't understand the tattoos. She would have to find a doctor who didn't know Mother. Maybe she could find the tattoo artist who did this to her, and he could tattoo over the marks on her hands with the color of her flesh.

An idle thought occurred to her—what would she say her name was? She hadn't been to town in ages, and no one would remember her there. They might laugh at the name Two. She was Two, just as her older brother was One and her younger brother was Three. Mother claimed to have given them other birth names, very long names that no one had ever used, but she loved nicknames and shortcuts.

One's calling was to be a missionary, and Three's calling was to be a professor. Mother could read people's destinies in their faces, and those were the respective destinies of One and Three. No one had seen One since he had boarded a ship for his first missionary outpost on a distant island that Mother had nick-named Heaven Island, but Mother assured everyone that she received a letter from him every year when a cargo ship made its annual voyage to the island and managed to pick up mail on its way. She wouldn't show anyone the letters, though, because she said they were meant for her eyes alone. Three (known professionally as Dr. Trois) excelled in his position at the college in town, where students found him interesting and his fellow professors found him witty, and he had dinner with Two and Mother once a month. Could she find Three and ask him for help now? She had no reason to believe he would keep any of her secrets. He had his own life, and he was polite to Mother when he visited, but he revealed little about himself except good news about his profession. Mother had foreseen he would never marry, and most likely he hadn't, but Two couldn't be certain. Who knew what went on in town?

Finally, the long stretch of road and trees gave way to scattered buildings, and she could see the center of town with its beige brick church tower and bells presiding in the distance. She began to worry people would think she looked strange. She didn't know what the style was in town. She was wearing a dress made of brown gauzy fabric threaded with silver, and another dress of thick purple wool underneath, and she suspected it was out-of-fashion. Finally, she saw a man in the distance wearing a gray jumpsuit and a matching plastic hat that looked like a close haircut. He was facing away from her, walking towards the center of town. She was determined to catch up with him, trotting as fast as she could in her heavy boots. As she passed him, she pretended to trip, thrusting herself forward onto the rough pavement, and her cry of pain was real.

"Are you all right?" He tended to her, thumping away the gravel pressed into her hands. His eyes were kind. He, too, wore gloves, thin and flexible ones that matched his outfit.

"I'm sorry to bother you," she said. What was he hiding under his gloves?

He used his gloved hands to briefly hover over her face and body.

"You seem to be all right." He smiled slightly without revealing his teeth, and he pulled her to her feet.

"Thank you so much. I tripped because I was in a hurry, and I'm a little lost?" "Where are you trying to go?" When she read romantic novels, she never pictured the leading male with a cherubic face and fiery eyes and gray gloved hands, and so she was inclined to think that he wasn't very handsome.

"I'm trying to find a doctor. Or a tattoo artist. Well...a doctor. No..." She held her reddening cheeks with her gloved hands to calm herself.

"I'm a doctor, though I'm not a tattoo artist. What's the trouble?"

"Can I trust you?""You can trust any doctor," he said with his close-lipped smile.

That wasn't what Mother had told her. But this was an emergency. She peeled her gloves off of her hands and displayed the tattoos, and as he examined them, she noticed new pictures on her hands. There was a tiny smiling face on the knuckle of her left middle finger, and a small bird silhouette and a purple sun (with radiating purple rays) on the back of her left hand, and a goldfish on her right thumb. Her palms were blank, fortunately. She imagined that tattooing her palms would be especially painful.

"These are interesting," he said. He frowned as he examined them.

"Please don't tell anyone. I fell asleep last night and woke up with these. I have no memory of obtaining them. It's the most terrifying thing that's ever happened to me."

"If you had gotten the tattoos last night, they'd be inflamed this morning. But these seem to have healed nicely. Did you try washing them off?"

"I washed my hands this morning."

"Let me take you into my office so you can really scrub them."

He led her to his white office building where the ceilings and walls had a plastic sheen that reminded her of an old pair of boots in her closet. Helpless as a child or sheep, she followed him down a silent corridor.

"Where is everyone?" she said.

He looked back at her, surprised. "Well, of course the office is closed. Today is a holiday."

"What holiday?"

"You're funny! It's the harvest celebration—you know. Surplus Day. I was on my way to the carnival."

He led her to a small bathroom at the end of the hall and gestured towards a bottle by the sink was filled with bright pink liquid. He watched her as she scrubbed and scrubbed her hands with the soap, cycling through dozens of washes. The tattoos didn't fade in the slightest. After what seemed like a very long time, she looked up and saw the mixture of sympathy and impatience on his face.

"What do I do?" she said.

"You asked for a doctor or a tattoo artist. You've tried the doctor, and it didn't work. Now we can look for a tattoo artist. There is always a tattoo booth at the carnival. That way we can kill two birds with one stone, since I had hoped to go to the carnival."

As she had followed him into the empty building, she now followed him outside and towards the center of town. She seemed to have so few options, and she couldn't think of what to do. It was close to nine, and Mother might arrive at her estate at moment to discover her missing, which could lead her to call the police or alert her husband or do any number of embarrassing things. Surely it wasn't illegal for Two to have tattoos without Mother's permission? Mother could make life hard for her, though. She shivered to think of what Mother would say.

The doctor smiled kindly at her and asked her questions about her life. He seemed both disturbed and impressed to hear how she lived.

"What a charmed life, in a way," he said. He told her about his busy practice, how he only took off for three holidays a year, and how much fun the carnival was, and how incredible it was that she never went to town, that she had never seen the carnival.

"I wish I were seeing it under happier circumstances," she said.

Soon they met a large crowd of people who were rushing past a cluster of thick trees. When Two and the doctor reached a break in the trees, they saw an open field full of giant machinery, the whole place dripping with delight and screams and giving off the smell of meat and sweets. She heard buzzes and dings that were like her doorbell but amplified twenty times. It was intriguing and disturbing. She hoped she had enough money in her pocketbook to pay the tattoo artist to fix her hands.

"You know, I bet you could work there if you wanted! You could work at the tattoo booth or on one of the rides. See, look!" He pointed to the wiry, muscular men and women who seemed hard at work at the carnival, and she saw what he meant. All of their flesh was almost covered with pictures. She looked down sadly at her own hands. Whose pictures had been drawn there? Who had chosen them?

"I'm sorry," the doctor said. "I was making a joke, but clearly it wasn't funny. You're in real trouble here."

"I appreciate your help. You've been very helpful," she said.

He led her down a long row of tents and small open-air rooms that held toys and games and foods she had never seen before, but she wasn't tempted to try anything. What if she had to work somewhere like this once Mother found out about her hands? Maybe this would be her only option. Unless the doctor would let him work for her. Since apparently doctors wore gloves, she would be able to cover her tattoos and blend in.

"Here it is," the doctor said, stopping her in front of a bright purple tent with the words "Skin Stamper" painted above the entryway.

The tattoo artist was a very small woman whose arms and hands and neck were exposed, displaying her array of tattooed vines winding around skeletons, bears juggling apples, and birds flying through watery skies.

"Why hello! Which of you beautiful people wants to remember this day forever? Or do you want couple tattoos? I've got a book full of things couples like...birds and hearts and calligraphy that could say anything—the day you met, today's date, a quote, or a simple message like I love you. Or love. Or love dearly. Or love forever. What are you thinking?"

Two was tired, and the thought of amassing more tattoos overwhelmed her into tears.

"Oh no, hon! Don't worry. It won't hurt like you think it will." The woman held up an elegant machine. "They're fast and almost painless these days."

"How long do tattoos take to heal, in your experience?" asked the doctor.

"About twenty-four hours."

"I see. Well, go ahead. Show her your hands," said the doctor, who had never asked Two for her name.

She displayed them, feeling mortified. "I didn't choose these designs. I would have never chosen any of these."

"I'm impressed by the detail. Whoever did these must be a hell of an artist. Who was it?"

"I went to sleep in my bed around nine or ten, and I'd had nothing alcoholic to drink, and then...I woke up like this."

The tattoo artist's eyes widened, but she continued to hold Two's hands and examine each intricate design.

"Can you fix it?" Two's hands shook with the effort of asking the question.

"Fix it?"

"Could you cover over the design with the color of my skin? Make it look like it never happened?"

"I'd be afraid to do it. It's not at all easy to match someone's flesh color over such a big area. Hand tattoos have always been tricky for me anyway. I can refer you to a girl in Clover. She's closed today, of course, but she could probably see you sometime this week. She's a real expert, and it can be tough to get an appointment, but if you call tomorrow and explain, she'd probably help you out. She's very nice."

"That would take too long," Two whispered. "So you're sure you can't do it? Please? You can't try?"

"I'm so sorry, darling. I'd just mess it up, I know I would."

The doctor led Two out of the tent and hugged her close while she wept and while the carnival workers shouted at her with words she couldn't quite make out. He led her out past the giant machines and wild laughter and incessant noise of every kind and helped her sit down in a soft tuft of grass at the edge of the field. She put her gloves back on her hands and held her covered fingertips to her eyes and wept.

"I'm so sorry," he said.

"It's okay."

"They're really nice tattoos, I think."

"Thank you."

"What else can I do to help?"

"Nothing. Please. Go and enjoy the carnival."

"Well...well. All right. Maybe just for an hour. But when I'm done, I'll come right back and check on you. Just sit here and cry it out, and think of what you want to do. I'll be back."

He darted away from her, across the grass and back to the carnival. Maybe he would come back. Maybe he would give her a job in his office. Still, she cried and cried and felt as if she'd been through an earthquake that had split her up the middle. Her tears blurred the images. She tried to imagine there were different pictures on her hands, like a river full of otters, or a charging bull, or a juggling bear like the one the tattoo artist had. Anything would be better than the tawdry jumble of images there. What had happened to her wasn't right, wasn't fair.

A rustle in the trees and grass behind her made her heart freeze. She turned her head and saw Mother approaching, her face grim, her arms extended. She was wearing her most elegant green muslin dress with button-up boots. Her hair was full of pouf and gathered in a knot on the top of her head. This was how she dressed for company.

Two shrieked and began to get to her feet to run away, but instead, she changed her mind and collapsed onto the grass to cry and beat her fists like a child.

"Dear, what made you come this way?" her mother said calmly.

"My hands—" Two began.

"But what made you think they could help you here?"

"I was afraid you'd be angry."

Mother sat down on the grass beside her, and Two was slightly touched that Mother would jeopardize the cleanliness of one of her best dresses for Two's sake.

"Are you angry?"

Mother shook her head slowly. "You see, you can't control all your desires. Sometimes they seep through. But I wanted you to know. I wanted you to feel, to know the cost, but be spared the consequences. Look at your hands now."

Two pulled off her gloves and was amazed to see her hands were healed, were blank again, were the color of her own flesh. The unwanted pictures were gone.

"Why did you do this to me? What were you trying to teach me with this horrible day and these awful tattoos?" she asked Mother.

"What do you think I was trying to teach you?" "Where is my husband? Where is my father?"

"Somewhere safe. They're somewhere else so we can be safe."

Mother was strong. Around them, the trees fidgeting and changed, dropped their dead parts, prepared for the cold. But with Mother, Two didn't have to worry about how she would survive the winter. Mother's preparations were invisible, her dead parts reabsorbed into her flesh, her reach unbelievably vast. Mother didn't leave town for business or pleasure. Mother sat with her on the grass. Mother kept her hands clean.

At home that afternoon, Helen gave them a late lunch, and Two and Mother spent the afternoon debating over samples of wallpaper for the dining room. Two liked the sapphire background covered with lush vines, but Mother preferred the ochre background covered with pale pink flowers. Choosing between them would surely take all winter.

Originally published in Vastarien

Author Note:
Over and over and over again, I write my own claptrap version of The Castle. But I enjoy doing it. There are always more towns down the road, some you remember passing through, and some where you once lived. Some have streets of gold, and some are loud and crowded. My instinct is to believe we all find peace eventually, but in the meantime, we must endure many absurdities. To pass the time, though, there is wallpaper.

Sisyphus and Jane Austen

Out of nowhere, the gods altered my punishment. A woman replaced my boulder, and I watched her roll.

"Why are you here?" I said.

"For a laugh." Her hair was the color of honey and almonds. I felt so hungry.

My boulder had been altered a number of times. The gods had made it larger for a few revolutions. When it slowed me down, they reduced it. On five or six occasions, the boulder changed into men, all of them strangers. They had all begged to meet me, and the gods had favored them. I am an interesting person in the underworld, it seems. But the boulder had never become a woman before her.

I had imagined many different beautiful women with me, usually helping me roll the boulder. Receiving any woman in any form meant the gods were smiling on me.

"You wanted to laugh at me," I said without condemnation. I was not surprised. I do not expect much.

"I asked to talk to you. I thought the gods would let me walk up and down with you and chat. But the gods are tricky devils."

I tried to push gently since her back was softer than stone. "The gods are clever." I had enough trouble with the gods without blaspheming them.

"They wanted to laugh at me," she said.

"They have laughed at me for some time. May their names be praised." I felt, I feel, some pity for myself.

"Oh yes, for thousands of years," she said, cavalier. She did not seem to feel sorry for me.

"I apologize. I cannot control my movements. I do not want to send a woman tumbling," I said before she rolled down again.

When I caught up to her, she laughed. "I'm all right. I feel no pain now. Do you?"

There were times I forgot about pain, but at long intervals, I would be surprised when the gods pricked me, their doll, with distant pins.

"I am not sure what is real. The gods play with me," I said.

"This isn't as fun as I'd hoped," she said. I felt forlorn. She was beginning to pity me, which meant she would soon grow tired of me.

"You knew my plight. You came to mock me." It felt good to argue with someone again. I was too fond of the boulder, my longest companion, to disagree with it.

"I came for wisdom, too. I thought you would have profound thoughts to share after all this time and work," she said at the top of the hill.

I considered my store of wisdom as I watched her roll and ran down the hill to meet her. She sat at the bottom, curled into a helpless ball.

"Wisdom about what?" I said as I pushed her.

"Like whether you regret your life, given the consequences." She turned towards me. Eyes like olives. No, I was not really hungry. I simply wanted to eat.

I did not answer. I could not think. We reached the top.

"Will you kiss me?" she said. It was time for her to roll.

When I reached the bottom, before the push, I was permitted a moment (the gods allowed it, praise the gods) to brush my lips against hers. They were so warm.

"You are so cold," she said as I pushed her to the top again. She shivered before she rolled.

The next time, she began her farewells.

"Thank you for the visit," she said.

"I do not have the power to grant visits." I am honest.

"Still. Thank you for your time. I hope you are...I hope you are happy."

One more glimpse of her hair, the sun playing through the strands. And she was a boulder again.

I was sorry to lose her, yet the boulder has comforts. I know its familiar weight and every pock and dimple. I looked up at the sky as the boulder fell, an act I often forget I am permitted.

"It was a nice visit," I told the boulder as we ascended. "But it's good to see you again."

Originally published in Daily Science Fiction

Author Note:
I can't remember how I felt when I wrote this, but I was probably sad! I was puzzling over what happiness is...is it remembering

to look up at the sky? Learning to love the boulder? Maybe. I was hoping for a more impressive answer, though.

Questions

& Answers

How ambitious are you in your writing career?

I don't want writing to feel like a job. I love it too much. That limits my ambition! I want to do things that come organically, and I don't want to push myself to do stuff I hate, like public speaking. I don't want to force myself to write something that wasn't my idea or that I'm not enjoying. I'm happy with how things are now. I am very ambitious in the sense that I want to produce what I consider to be the best possible version of what I can do. Fortunately, that's a life's work, and it doesn't depend on anyone else.

Do you see yourself settling into being a novelist first in the future, or do you think short stories will always play a major role in your writing?

I felt like I had to write novels when I started writing fiction, because I love novels so much. I deeply love short stories, too, but novels have been some of my best friends. And yet, writing novels doesn't come as naturally to me as writing short stories. I have a draft of one novel that I'm happy with that I hope to keep polishing. I'll probably play around with more novels in the future. But shorts are more fun for me at this point.

Is there a genre you've yet to fully tackle that you could see yourself writing one day?

I enjoy mysteries so so much. I've tried writing them before, but they always end up weird. Maybe someday I can write a true traditional mystery tale, or at least one that's somewhat more faithful to the genre. I have my doubts that I could! But it would be fun.

Do you tell people in your day-to-day life that you're a writer? (I admit, I don't often reveal that I'm a writer or publisher...)

I generally don't. It's my passion, but like any passion, it's not going to interest everyone. Some people live for golf, but I don't have much to contribute to conversations about it. So it's hard to talk about writing with someone who doesn't really care about it, or who cares about it in a different way than I do. I know it's not that important in the grand scheme of things, but it's extremely important to me, and I don't want to annoy other people or myself with unsatisfying conversations about it.

I know you have some future releases that have already been announced, what can you tell our readers about them?

First, I want to thank Matthew Stott and *Tales from Between* for the opportunity to make *Grime Time*...I've had a great experience working with him, and I hope to read more collections from *Tales from Between* in the future, including one by Matthew himself! I've loved the previous offerings from Ai Jiang, Elin Olausson, and Samantha Kolesnik, and I appreciate the idea of taking small helpings of a writer's work to enjoy. There are so many writers whose work I love in this community, as well as great writers I have yet to discover, and I look forward to seeing them in these pages!

Next year, I plan to release a novella called *Star Shapes* and a short story collection called *Glass Stories*. *Star Shapes* is a Southern Gothic story about a girl in her twenties who is kidnapped from downtown Birmingham, Alabama, and taken to the country by an odd family. She has to figure out why they kidnapped her, which has to do with a homemade book of constellations and a strange set of beliefs.

Glass Stories is a collection of all my stories featuring glass, like "Glass Book," "Glass Pet," "Glass Mountain," and so on. Glass this and glass that. Why glass? It was a way for me to explore the spirit, that which can't be seen. Some of the stories are very weird spinoffs of fairy tales. Some take place in Alabama. Some are earnest and some are unserious. While revising them, I will admit that I've enjoyed rereading them.

The
Food
Fellow

L ike many tragedies, mine began slowly. Like few tragedies, it started at the grocery store.

Before, in the beginning, I visited the Food Fellow closest to my apartment every third day. Every blessed third day (barring a highly unusual out-of-town trip or illness), I'd drop in after work. A million factors made those visits comforting...their regularity, the stark familiarity of the florescent lights, the friendly cartoon faces on the cereal boxes, the gentle fountain spraying the produce at intervals, and much more. And the store never closed. The store was the only thing that catered to me instead of the other way around.

I'm very giving. As a dental office receptionist, I always comforted the most nervous patients on the phone and took their questions about receding gum lines and tooth decay. I googled their questions and gave the answers a positive spin, and the patients always felt better. Also, even though my boyfriend and I worked the same hours, I did most of the cooking for us. We took turns cooking for a while, but he always made frozen pizza when it was his turn, so I took over.

Before things got weird, I never spoke to any of the clerks who worked at the Food Fellow. I recognized most of them in a vague sort of way, like someone you might wave to in a dream. There was the tall guy with wild red hair in charge of the shopping carts, the tiny, tiny lady who bagged groceries, the nondescript butcher whose face I never saw (since he was always sorting and examining meat), and a shifting group of teenagers who stocked. There were others, but those stuck out in my mind. It was a rainy day in September when I first met the Produce Manager. Or rather, I didn't officially meet him, but we noticed each other.

I was knotting the plastic bag for my cucumbers when he wheeled over his cart of sweet potatoes and began stacking them in the next aisle. On grocery days, I would leave work fifteen minutes early to avoid the dinnertime rush. I liked maintaining a certain distance from other people in the grocery store, a certain luxurious space to deliberate about which avocado was the most precious or whether caramel-flavored coffee or donut-flavored coffee would bring me the most joy. Still, I needed sweet potatoes, so I tore off another produce bag and crept beside the man. I expected to be politely ignored, but instead he paused his potato-sorting to turn my way. He stared at me as I chose two sweet potatoes to steam for dinner. I was too flustered to choose the smoothest ones, and I ended up with two that were uncharacteristically misshapen.

Why was he staring at me? After I moved away to choose my bananas, I stared at the back of his head, at the long, salt-and-pepper locks matted down beneath his store cap. Was he attracted to me? Was he judging me? I texted my boyfriend about the incident, but he didn't respond. He told me on our first date that I was too dramatic, and that's been his attitude ever since.

I mostly dismissed the incident until my next visit. I was making vegetable soup that night and salad for the next day's lunch, so I had a long list of produce to gather. I was distracted. My boss had yelled at me for staying so long on the phone with some patients that other patients couldn't get through to make their appointments. I felt indignant to be scolded for working so hard, and anyway, he didn't have to yell about it. As I tried to block the day out of my mind, I pictured miniature patients pushing themselves through the tiny holes in the phone receiver, corkscrewing their way into the office and running around jubilantly. Sampling toothpaste and playing with the picks. Yes, they wanted to get through, but I was attending to patients with a different set of problems.

And so the produce man took me by surprise again, gently stacking kiwis like they were freshly-laid eggs. And kiwis happened to be on my list. I didn't want to disturb him, though. This time, I noticed a pin on his hat that said "Produce Manager." I chose the other fruits and vegetables on my list and lingered in the aisles considering expensive fruits I'd never tried before, like dragon fruits and kumquats. Still, he kept arranging and rearranging kiwis. I thought of what my boyfriend would say and reminded myself I was being ridiculous. My boyfriend loved kiwis, after all, and he wouldn't understand if I didn't bring them home. I got up the courage to creep near the produce man to choose the kiwis farthest from his hand.

This time, there was nothing subtle about the way he looked at me. He turned his whole head and stared, his face frozen like a mask, his eyes glittering under the florescent lights.

"I'm sorry," I said. He didn't reply. He kept his hands on as many kiwis as he could, as if he were a chicken and had laid them himself and couldn't bear to part with them. I tried to avoid looking directly at his face. I had gotten close enough to the kiwis this time to get my hands on a few of them before scuttling away. What a strange, strange man! I decided if my boyfriend complained about the dearth of kiwis, I would tell him to go to the store and get some himself. In fact, he did complain when I returned with a limp bag containing just two kiwis, and I told him what had happened, and he rolled his eyes at me. He thought I'd imagined everything.

Three days later, I returned to the store, this time quite anxious, but determined to conquer my fear. I went straight for the produce section, and to my relief, the Produce Manager wasn't there. I filled a bag full of kiwis. It was a boom time, and I was going to enjoy it. And yet when I got another bag to fill with onions, I turned back around to find the produce man stacking the very things. He'd snuck up on me. And how could I make it through the week without onions? I waited in the produce section for a moment, hoping another shopper would wander that way so I had moral support. No one came my way, though. I was always left alone with the Produce Manager. He caressed the skins of his onions as he stacked them, regarding them as giant pearls.

You see, I never complain about workers to their bosses, because I know what it's like when someone complains about me.

That's when I get yelled at, made to feel small because I'm a small part of the boss's operation and not so vital that I have to be cared for. I don't want to do that to someone else. I had no idea what the Food Fellow's Manager looked like, and I knew I couldn't bring myself to ask for him. I snuck up behind the Produce Manager, hoping to pop out and scare him for a change when I reached for my onions. Once I crept quite close to him, he turned around and surprised me instead. I shrieked and dropped my bag. He fixed his paralyzing glare on me, and I realized his previous looks had been muted like the sun behind the clouds. Now his flashlight glare was on me, and I couldn't move even to pick up the bag I had dropped. I felt like I was shaking, and I realized nonsense sounds were escaping my mouth. After what must have been a full minute of staring at me reproachfully, he broke the spell by grabbing the plastic bag from the floor and tossing it into the trash can affixed to his produce cart. He turned away from me and began playing with the onions again.

I felt so stupid then to have been scared. Panicking by the onions! I realized he must be trying to tell me something. Was plastic the problem? Maybe he was illustrating to me that by putting my produce in plastic, I was creating more and more trash that would exist longer than I would. Grabbing them constantly and then tossing them out, my used bags numerous as stars in the sky. I had noticed on other trips that the store sold little canvas bags that could be reused for fruit and vegetables. I had noticed other shoppers, mostly women who seemed to work from home, wielding such thoughtful products. I persisted, and I choose three canvas bags on display near the greens to buy at the checkout. I decided to experiment.

Boldly, I approached again. I walked this time, pretended to be calm, though my heart leapt into my throat as I neared the man. I grabbed an onion and stuffed it in my sack before he turned around again.

"What do you want?" They were his first words to me, and they were growled rather than spoken.

My cheeks felt hot. I had every right to be there! It was my Food Fellow.

"What do you think I want? I want onions like a normal person at a normal grocery store. And I want to choose them without being bothered. What do *you* want?" I felt the trembling joy of having told someone off succinctly and successfully.

"You've been watching me for days, stalking me like a wolf," he said. I could tell he was trying to sound innocent. His gravelly tone crept into his attempt to seem gentle, and his face of stone couldn't soften itself.

"Watching you? You stare at me whenever I try to buy something. Do you think I'm eating too much produce or something? Or not enough? Or is it the plastic that's the problem?"

"The problem?" he said, a note of fear in his voice. Briefly, he seemed distracted, and I was able to examine his face. It was pale, and gray stubble lined his cheeks, and his eyes were blue and sorrowful. He seemed so innocent in that moment.

What happened next is something no one has believed, so I rarely tell it anymore. A light shone on his face, a ghastly angelic light. People tell me a florescent light must have flickered overhead at that moment and given the false impression. But in that moment, to me, the light revealed he had eyes like a reptile—cold and lidless and sick, with misshapen irises. I screamed again.

"I'm getting the Store Manager," he said, hurrying away. When he left me, I filled my new canvas bag with as many onions as it could hold—seven onions. I knew in my heart this would be the last day I would go to the Food Fellow. I felt like I was stocking up for the apocalypse.

The tiny, tiny woman bagged my groceries indifferently, and in the distance, the Produce Manager and the Store Manager watched me. They stood beside the sweet potatoes and conferred, the Produce Manager stroking his stubble and the Store Manager half-pointing his finger at me. I was terrified. Would they call the police? What was my crime? Or what they track me down at my home and attack me?

I took my eyes off of them as I loaded my bags in my cart, so I was surprised when they overtook me and blocked my exit. They stood in front of the automatic door, and I looked helplessly out the window at the gray wet streets mottled with red taillights. I dug in my purse for my phone to call the police or my boyfriend, but the Security Guard walked up behind me, which startled me and made me drop the phone in one of my bags. I turned around and saw that he was a tremendous man, his head reaching almost to the height of the exit sign.

"I need to speak to you in private, Miss," he said.

The security room was surprisingly comfortable, with a red sofa and a well-watered potted plant. The Security Guard hovered over me, pacing, and he told me that the Produce Manager had caught me shoplifting.

"What? Shoplifting what?" I said.

In a flash, like a striking cobra, he reached into my coat pocket and pulled out a dragon fruit.

"I didn't take that!" I objected, but I knew it wouldn't help. They were working together, working against me. They had planted that fruit in my coat pocket for their own purposes.

"The Produce Manager saw you take it." His voice was sweeter than the Produce Manager's, but it was wiser too.

"Call the police then," I said, hoping I was calling his bluff.

"I'd be happy to. The police chief is a friend of mine." He smiled at me.

I wasn't sure if he was telling the truth, but I was afraid to risk it. I could see that luck wasn't with me that day. I hung my head and didn't answer.

"But there's an alternative," he said. He held the dragon fruit in his palm like it was living. "You could eat it right here. Then it would be a store sample. Nothing illegal about that."

"Oh," I said. Tears formed in my eyes. What was the goal of these three men? I couldn't understand it.

The produce manager and store manager came into the room to join the Security Guard, and the produce manager carried a paper plate and a knife. He cut open the fruit while the two other men watched, and he arranged slices of the black-and-white fruit on the paper plate and brought it to me like he was my servant.

"You try some too," I said.

He smiled his ice smile, and I watched him crush a slice with his long teeth. Now it was my turn. I picked up a slice, tried to make peace with death if it was my time to die, and ate. It tasted like summer, and I have to admit I enjoyed it.

"That was good?" the Produce Manager said.

"You're a loyal customer. We didn't want to call the police," the Store Manager said.

"We all know you. You come in every third day," the Security Guard said.

"Can I leave now?" I said.

"Yes, if you promise to come back, and to never steal again," the Store Manager said. He lowered the glasses I hadn't noticed until that moment and gave me a clear view of his swamp-green eyes.

They were all oldish men. I figured I could come back some day in the distant future, could come back after they had all died. So I promised. What other choice did I have?

They escorted me outside, the three of them, so closely their skin kept brushing against my skin. I took my bags home and left them on the counter for my boyfriend to unpack. When I told him what had happened, he seemed mystified at first, but he said I must have put the fruit in my pocket by accident. The next day, he told me it was all right if I had stolen the fruit, but that I should tell him the truth.

"You don't need to steal fruit," he said. "If you can't afford something and want it, I'll pay extra for it."

I shook my head. I hadn't put that fruit in my pocket. I simply hadn't wanted it. Once I had tasted it, sure, I realized how nice it was. But now it was associated with a bad memory, so I didn't want to eat it again.

My boyfriend would seem to forget about the incident from time to time. I never forgot, so I was never surprised when he brought it up at random intervals. The men at the store wanted me to try the fruit they had accused me of stealing, but they never asked me why I stole it. My boyfriend was obsessed with the question.

After several weeks of random questioning (during which time I patronized a slightly more remote grocery store called Meal Deals), I realized I couldn't take it anymore. It was like I was living with the Produce Manager. He was obsessed with me and obsessed with the fruit I had supposedly wanted to eat. Before, he had barely cared what I thought. Now he was watching my every move, straining to hear every syllable, all so he could figure out what drove me to commit my alleged crime.

I left him. I asked my boss for a raise, didn't get one, and took an extra nighttime job at a bakery so I could comfortably pay my own rent. I moved to the other side of the city, and I paid a little extra to have my groceries delivered. At the bakery, sometimes I catch someone swiping a donut or a muffin from the glass case by the door, wrapping it in a napkin, stuffing it in their purse or pocket. But I look the other way. The manager doesn't notice. I know I'm not a model employee.

Sometimes I wonder if it's worth it. If I advance to manager myself someday, maybe I can return to the Food Fellow with my head high. I suspect, though, that I'll forget my self-esteem when I go back, that whether the Produce Manager is there or not, I'll still feel his spirit hovering over the onions and kiwis.

Originally published in Vastarien

Author Note:

I didn't think anyone would ever accept this weird story, and I was grateful and surprised when Jon Padgett accepted it for Vastarien. I think that was the first time I felt like I fit in with a group of writers, that I sort of belonged somewhere. On a personal note, I hate going to the grocery store.

SUPPORT

Join our Patreon and get everything we publish: patreon.com
/TalesFromBetween

MORE TO READ

TFBPRESENTS

1- Ai Jiang's Smol Tales From Between Worlds

2- Elin Olausson's Shadow Paths

3- Samantha Kolesnik's Lonesome Haunts

OTHER RELEASES

Tales From Between: A Strange Literary Journal

Tales From Between: Words & Pictures